BOB

Anne Appert

HARPER
An Imprint of HarperCollinsPublishers

This is B ob.

Hi!
Actually, it's
Blob. With an L.

PAINT

For Mom and Dad.
Thanks for
supporting me
no matter who
I choose to be.

Blob
Copyright © 2021 by Anne Appert
All rights reserved. Manufactured in Italy.
No part of this book may be used or reproduced in any manner whatsoever without written permission except in the case of brief quotations embodied in critical articles and reviews. For information address HarperCollins Children's Books, a division of HarperCollins Publishers, 195 Broadway, New York, NY 10007.
www.harpercollinschildrens.com

ISBN 978-0-06-303612-3

The artist used Procreate to create the digital illustrations for this book.
Typography by Chelsea C. Donaldson
21 22 23 24 25 RTLO 10 9 8 7 6 5 4 3 2 1

First Edition

Bob is a creature of indeterminate kind.

Bob has a unique talent.

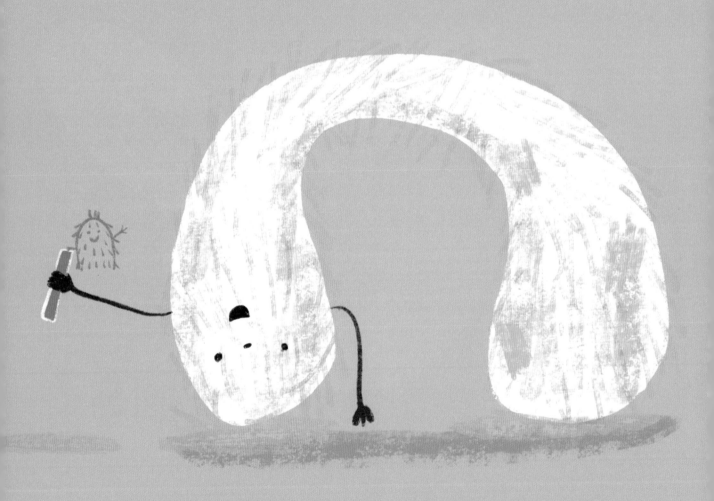

As a blob, Bob can be whatever
animal you want.

Yes. Any animal.

Or a mouse.

Bob can be a giraffe,

Well, that's a stretch.

an elephant,

I'll never forget things!

a unicorn,

They're mythical, one of a kind! Hey, can we be sure I'm not already a unicorn?

and an octopus too.

AN OCTOPUS? Do I have enough legs?

Bob can be a—

Okay, Bob.

Well?

What do you want to be?

Are you sure, Bob?

Interesting choice, Bob.

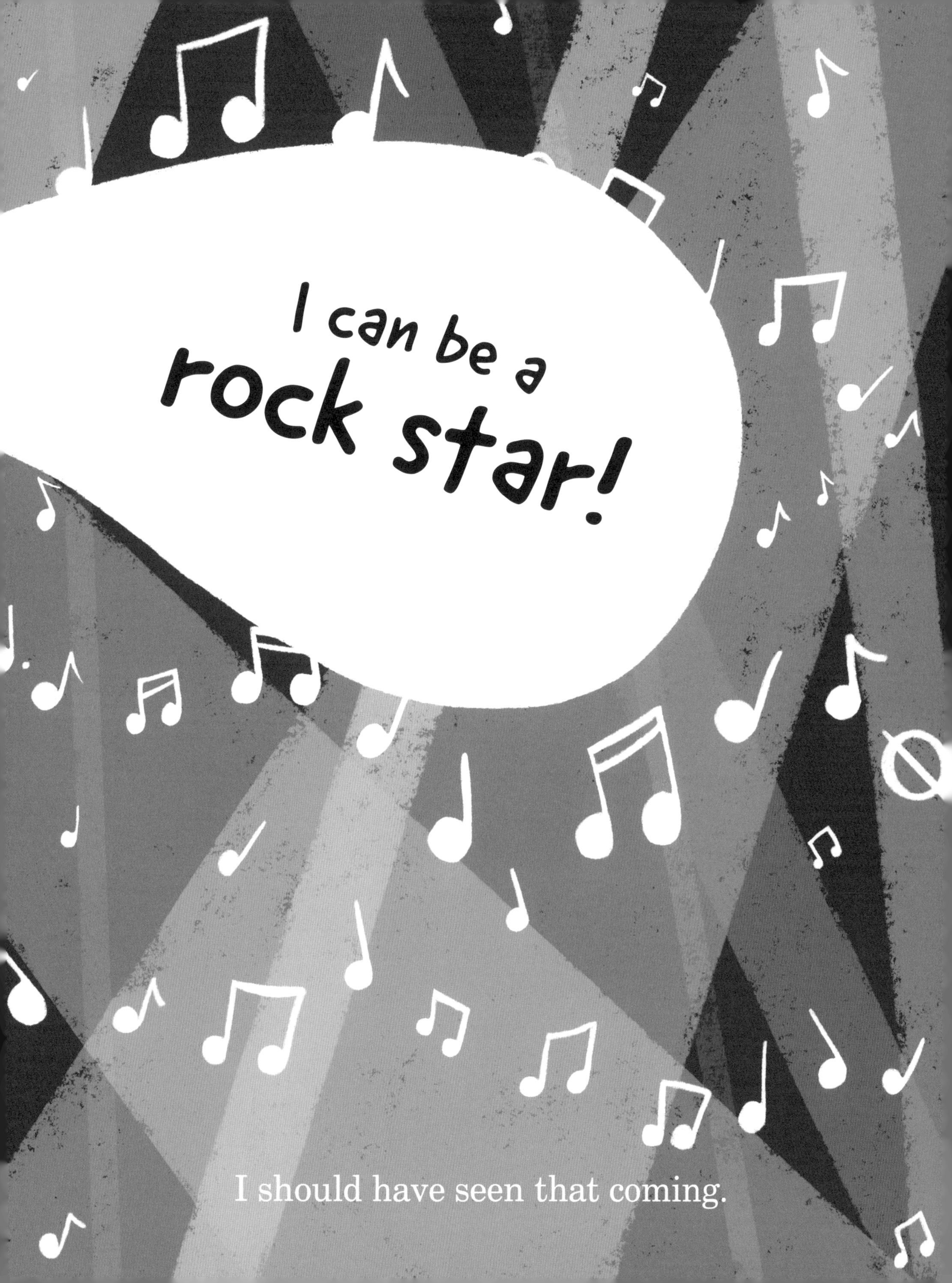

I should have seen that coming.

Anything else?

Well . . .
I can be a cloud.

Clouds are rather blobby.

A skydiver.

This octopus *definitely* has enough legs.

Now you're making hay with this.

What?

You can't decide?
But you can be anything!

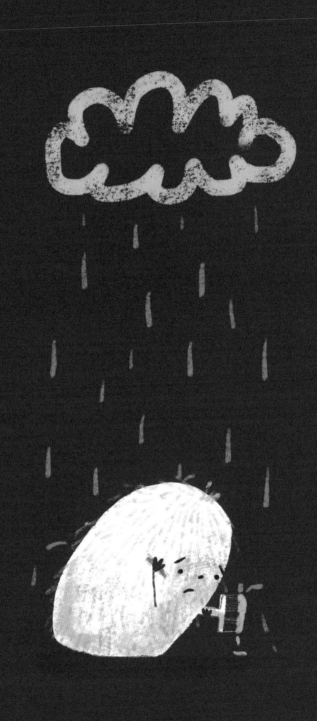

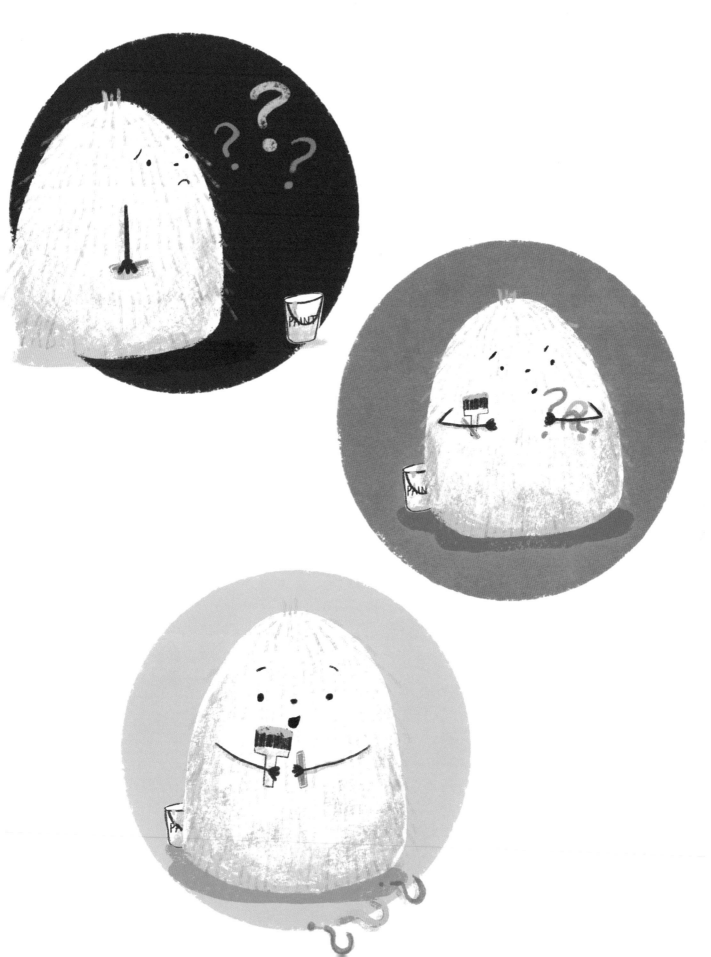

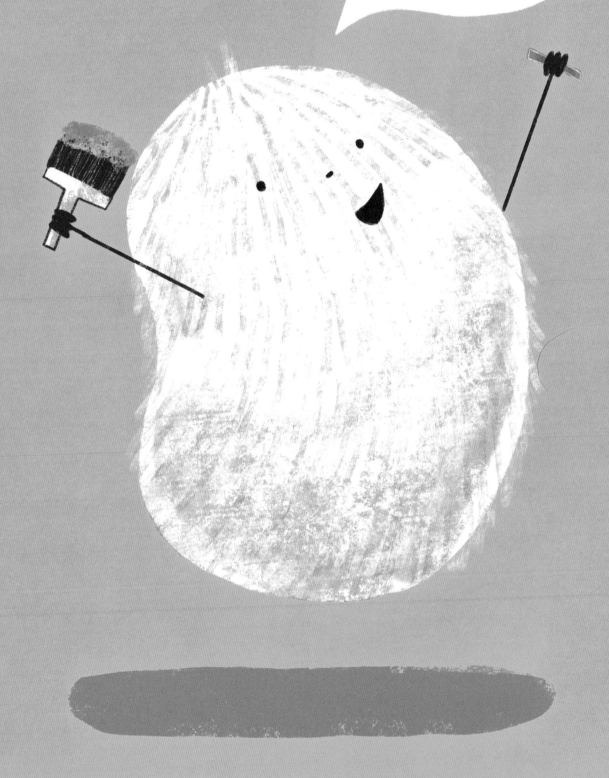

You decided, Bob?

Well, that begs the question:
What do blobs do?

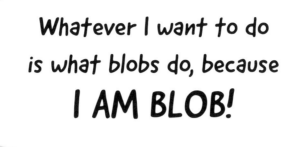

That sounds perfect, Blob.